Rachel Elliot

illustrated by

Karen Sapp

 D0230749

Wide Awake Jake

meadowside
CHILDREN'S BOOKS

Jake couldn't sleep.

He lay on his back.

He lay on his tummy.

He even lay upside down.
But it was **no** good.

He was **still**
wide awake.

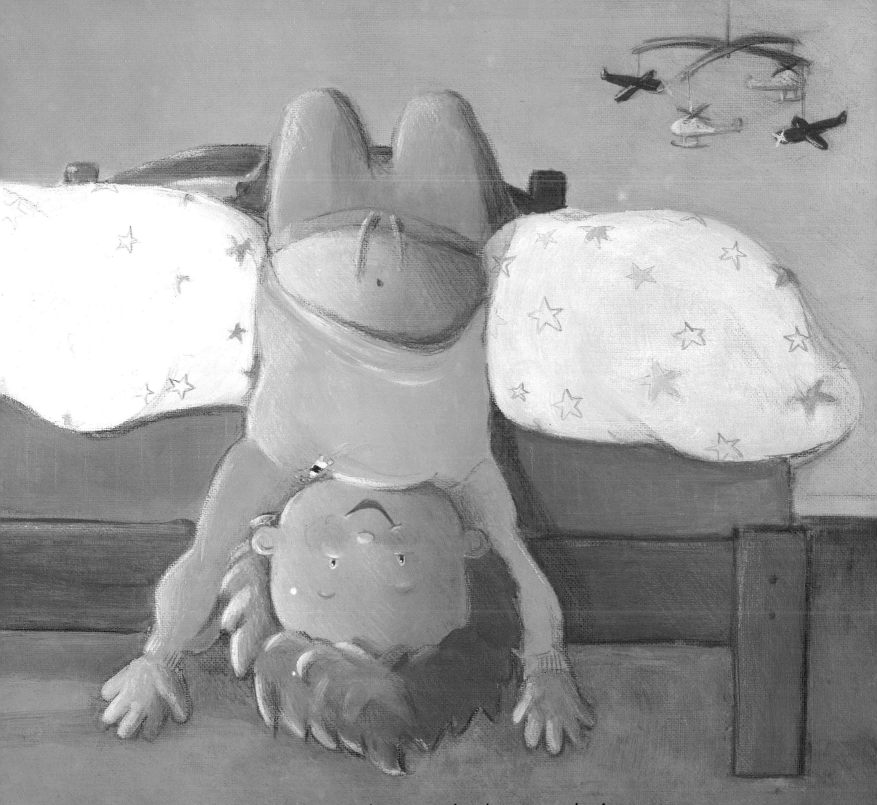

So Jake got up and went downstairs...

HUFF
PUFF
HUFFITY
PUFF

"I can't sleep," huffed Jake.

"Try counting sheep," said Dad.

But Jake didn't think **that** would help.

"Pretend you're a little bear,
going to sleep for the winter,"
said Mum.

Jake thought that **could** work.

So he went back upstairs...

pad

pad

pad

Jake curled up inside his blanket.

"I'm a little bear,

grrr, grrr,"

he growled.

But then he heard noises.

What if it was a great BIG bear?
It might have long, sharp claws
and huge, yellow teeth!

And his fur was very itchy.

Jake, the little bear,
was still wide awake.
So he got up

and went downstairs...

THUMP
BUMP
CLUMPITY
THUMP!

"I can't sleep," grumped Jake.

"Count to a million," said Dad.

Jake didn't think **that** would help.

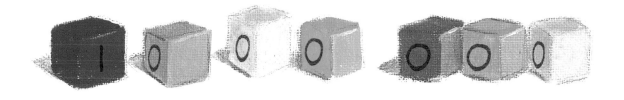

"Pretend you're a little mouse,
going to sleep in a mousehole,"
said Mum.

Jake thought that **could** work.

So he went back upstairs...

squeak

squeak

squeak

Jake crawled to the bottom of his bed.
But then he heard noises.
It might be a
big
fat
cat!

"Eek!" squeaked Jake,
the little mouse.
HURRY
FLURRY
SCURRY

"I can't sleep," worried Jake.

Dad just sighed.

Jake didn't think **that** was very helpful.

"Pretend you're a baby bird
in your nest,"
said Mum.

Jake thought it was worth a try.

So he went back upstairs...

flutter

flutter

flutter

Jake pulled his pillow under the covers.

"I'm a baby bird,
sitting in my nest,"
he whispered.

But his feathers kept

making him sneeze.

Then he
heard
noises!

Somebody was
pulling the
covers
down...

It was a big, hairy bear!

No, it didn't have any claws.

It was a fat, scary cat!

No, it didn't have a tail.

It was a big, scowly owl!

No, it didn't have a beak.

It was Mum!

Mum put the pillows straight.
She tucked Jake in,
nice and tight.

"You're my brave little Jake,
safe in your very own bed,"
said Mum.

"Now close your eyes.
It's time to sleep."

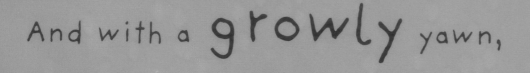

And with a growly yawn,

and a mouse-quiet wink,

and a fluttery blink,

Jake, the little boy,
was fast asleep.

For Mum and Robin
R.E.

For Grandad,
a special book for a special man
K.S.

First published in 2004
by Meadowside Children's Books,
185 Fleet Street, London EC4A 2HS

Text © Rachel Elliot 2004. Illustrations © Karen Sapp 2004.
The rights of Rachel Elliot and Karen Sapp to be identified
as the author and illustrator have been asserted by them
in accordance with the Copyright, Designs and Patents Act, 1988.

A CIP catalogue record for this book
is available from the British Library.
10 9 8 7 6 5 4 3 2
Printed in U.A.E